A Home for Sydney

by Danielle Caro
Illustrated by Nadia Ilchuk

Danielle Caro

Sydney

Book design by Jeanne Balsam
jeannebalsamgraphics.com

Library of Congress Number: 2019913621

Dedication

*A **Home for Sydney*** is dedicated to animal rescue volunteers.
They generously give their time and love to animals in need.
From animal handling & socializing, cage cleaning,
and administrative tasks, these people work to
save animals' lives and find them homes.

Sydney was a playful Saluki puppy. She lived with her mother and siblings on a farm outside the city of Dubai.

She loved to run in the desert. The sand felt warm under her paws.

Sydney would have been happy living here forever.

One day, a man
visited the farm.
He wanted to buy
a puppy to train
for racing.

He examined them
all closely and
chose Sydney.

Sydney didn't even
get to say goodbye.

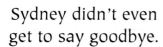

She arrived at a house
with a fenced-in yard.
She heard barking and
saw several Salukis
looking at her.

Her owner
placed her in the
yard to meet the
other dogs.

Each day, they were taken two or three at a time to an exercise pen and trained for racing. The pen had two circular paths around it. A rabbit was placed in the outer path so the dogs could see it, but not catch it.

Sydney watched the other dogs and learned to chase the rabbit.

After months of practice, Sydney was able to keep up with the rabbit.
Now Sydney could race with the other dogs on the sand track.

A big cash prize was given to the owner with the fastest Saluki.
Sydney loved running on the track and making her owner proud.

It was race day and the whistle blew!

Sydney was in the lead from the very start. Her eyes sparkled and her ears blew back in the wind. Her feet were a blur and her tail streamed behind her.

She approached the finish line and felt a pain in her back leg.

Her speed slowed and a dog passed her. And another.

Would this be the end of her racing career?

Sydney's owner no longer wanted her if she couldn't win races.

He drove her far away from home and abandoned her.

She was all alone and trembled.

It was getting dark and she got caught in some brush.

She squirmed and shook, but when she broke free,
her face and neck were scratched.

She found a safe spot to rest for the night.

Sydney woke up the next morning to the sound of footsteps.

She was frightened, but a man spoke softly and asked,
"Are you hungry?"

Sydney had no dinner the night before,
and her ears perked up thinking about food.

The man handed her a treat, and led her to his truck.

The truck stopped and they went inside.

"You will be well cared for here," he said.

A kind woman washed Sydney's scratches and took her outside to play.

Sydney met Sandy, Apollo, and Jasper. She loved their company and became close friends with Apollo. She felt safe and was happy during the short time she spent at the shelter.

One afternoon, she and the others were taken to an airport.

The dogs were boarded onto an airplane headed to New York City.

Sydney was stressed inside her crate. She scratched at the door and panted.

The dogs were greeted in New York by their foster mom, Emily.

She took them to her apartment.

"Tomorrow we will attend an adoption event. You will each have a chance to find your forever home," she said.

The next morning, Emily brought Sydney and the other dogs to the adoption event at Woof & Wash in New York.

The city was loud and busy.

Sydney began to whine. Apollo stood close by to comfort her.

Sydney was greeted by the Caro family.

They asked Emily questions about Sydney.

They loved how calm and gentle she was.

Mackenzie patted Sydney's head and she stopped whining.

Sydney was exactly what they had hoped for!

"Would you like to come home with us and be a part of our family?" they asked. Sydney wagged her tail.

She turned toward Apollo and gave him a nuzzle. She would miss her friend.

Sydney walked with the Caros to their car, and jumped inside.

She watched the city fade away.

They drove for a long while before finally stopping.

"We're home!" said Mackenzie.

Sydney jumped out of the car. She heard birds chirping, and saw trees and a lovely house.

"Let's go for a walk," her family said.

They returned home and Sydney stepped inside slowly.

Everyone watched to see her reaction.

Sydney explored the different rooms in the house and saw
a large bed in the kitchen.

"That's for you," Mackenzie told her.

Sydney was so excited that she leapt into it and rolled on her back.

Sydney knew she would be happy living here forever.

Author's Notes

Dubai is a city-state in the country United Arab Emirates (UAE). It is located in the Middle East on the continent of Asia. It is in the Arabian Desert where the weather is hot and dry.

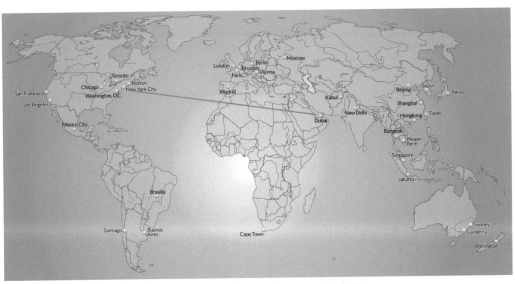

Sydney's journey from Dubai to New York City

The Saluki may be the world's oldest dog breed. They were the hunting hounds of kings for thousands of years. They are quick sprinters and love a good chase. Salukis are gentle, independent and loyal pets. They are the fastest dog breed over long distance runs. Salukis are still raced in the Middle East in UAE as well as in nearby Qatar, and cash prizes are awarded. They are usually raced till around the age of two. At that time, many are in need of new homes.

Sydney at home with the Caro family - a lovely example of the Saluki breed.

Acknowledgments

Nadia Ilchuk - Thank you for the beautiful illustrations. You brought my story to life.

Jeanne Balsam - Thank you for your expert editing and creative book design. Your guidance in putting everything together was invaluable.

Just4Kids - Thank you Loren and the Just4Kids writing group for your support while I wrote this book. You kept me motivated every step of the way.

My family - Thank you to my husband and children for your extra help at home while I spent many hours focused on my book.

My friends - Thank you to my friends for your encouragement and support. You all believed in me while I wrote my first book.

Biography

Danielle and Sydney

Danielle Caro is an animal lover and first-time author. She resides in Morris County, NJ with her husband, three children and their rescue dog, Sydney. Danielle grew up surrounded by animals of all sizes, from fish to horses. She is an animal advocate and a member of several animal welfare organizations.

Danielle has always had a passion for children's books. She enjoyed the many years spent reading as a child, as well as with her own children. She joined a local writer's group, Just4Kids, to learn more about writing a book of her own. The idea for her book came after bringing home their rescue dog, Sydney.

Made in the USA
Middletown, DE
17 April 2023